# OLYMPIC JOKES

## 100% UNOFFICIAL

# OLYMPIC JOKES

## 100% UNOFFICIAL

MACMILLAN CHILDREN'S BOOKS

Published 2021 by Macmillan Children's Books
an imprint of Pan Macmillan
The Smithson, 6 Briset Street, London EC1M 5NR
EU representative: Macmillan Publishers Ireland Limited,
Mallard Lodge, Lansdowne Village, Dublin 4
Associated companies throughout the world
www.panmacmillan.com

ISBN 978-1-5290-4302-0

1 3 5 7 9 8 6 4 2

A CIP catalogue record for this book is available from the British Library.
Compiled and Illustrated by Perfect Bound Ltd
Illustrated by Dan Newman

Printed and bound by CPI Group (UK) Ltd, Croydon CR0 4YY

# Contents

# Stadium Heroes

A shrimp came third in the 100m final.

**It got the prawns medal.**

An athlete dreamt someone was shouting, 'On your marks. Get set. Go!'

**She woke up with a start.**

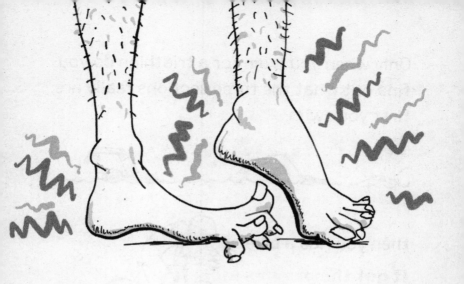

I had to give up the pentathlon. I was
great at most of the events, but running
hurt so much and I kept losing.

**I couldn't stand the agony of de-feet.**

What's harder to catch, the faster you run?

**Your breath.**

What do you call a pentathlete that can't sink?

**Bob.**

Only when you train for a triathlon do you find out what the three sections **really** are: first you swim,

then you ride a bike,

and finally you run . . .
out of money.

'How's the triathlon swim training going?'

   **'OK I suppose . . . the chlorine dries up my tears.'**

How can you tell if there's a triathlete in the room?

**Don't worry, he'll tell you.**

Who thinks triathletes are cool?

**Other triathletes.**

Hippos can swim faster than humans and run faster than humans.

**So your only chance to beat them is in the bike race.**

What do you call someone who isn't very good, but has a go at running, cycling and swimming?

**A try-athlete.**

'Guess what – I've got a personal trainer.'

   **'So what? I've got two of them – one on each foot.'**

What happened when the triathlete ran behind his trainer's car?

**He got exhausted.**

And what happened when he ran in front of the trainer's car?

**He got tyred.**

A triathlete crashed into a barrier during the cycle section, and got questioned by a medic.

'You seemed to be going quite fast – what gear were you in?'

**'Cycling shoes, a helmet and a swimming costume with a number on the back.'**

I can't stand discus.

**It makes me want to hurl.**

There's a new TV sports show which just shows hammer, shotput, javelin and discus competitions.

**It's called *Game of Throwns*.**

Did you hear about the athlete who cheated in the 100-metre sprint?

**He took a shortcut.**

Some athletes complained that one of the hurdles was too high.

**They'll get over it eventually.**

A high-jumper walks into a bar . . .

**He was disqualified.**

What is a runner's favourite school subject?

**Jog-raphy.**

How does a sprinter
remember to train?

**She jogs her memory.**

Did you hear the
joke about the bad
pole-vaulter?

**It never goes
over very well.**

How do sprinters like their boiled eggs?

**Runny.**

What do you call an unstoppable marathon runner?

**A jogger-naut.**

**'I'm thinking about running a marathon again.'**

'Wow, you've run a marathon before?'

**'No ... but I've thought about it.'**

Is Usain Bolt quicker during the day or at night?

**At night – he's fast asleep for seven hours.**

An athlete walked towards the stadium
with a long pole sticking out of his bag.

'Are you a pole vaulter?' asked a curious
spectator.

**'No, I'm a German,' said the athlete.**

My doctor says I've got the
body of an athlete.

**Well, the feet, anyway.**

Training properly for a marathon
is hard work.

**But it's worth it in the long run.**

A javelin thrower called Vicky
Found the grip of her javelin sticky.
When it came to the throw
She couldn't let go.
Which made judging the distance quite tricky.

Did you hear about the athlete who
can only win races in wet weather?

**He's the raining champion.**

What do athletes eat
before a race?

**Fast food.**

# Take Aim...

What does an archer get
when she hits a bullseye?

**A very angry bull.**

What makes an archer so accurate?
**Arrow-dynamics.**

A longbow can be used by left-handed and right-handed archers.

**It's am-bow-dextrous.**

What happened when Orion lost an archery match?

**He got a constellation prize.**

Have you ever tried blindfold archery?

**You don't know what
you're missing.**

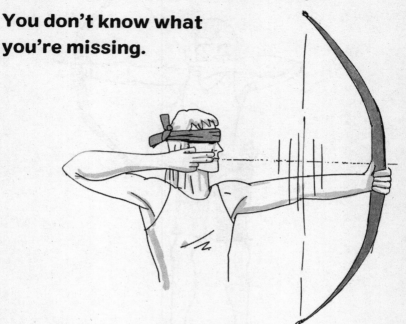

'How did you manage to get a place
on the archery team?'

   **'I had to pull a few strings.'**

I don't like that archer showing off about
how good they are.

**Very arrow-gant.**

How could you tell the archer was nervous?

**He was all a-quiver.**

What does a dog use for archery?

**A bow-wow.**

That archer has a strangely
smooth forehead.

**I think she's had bow-tox.**

Those two archers are very competitive.

**They're arch-enemies.**

What do you call an archer with no hair?

**Archibald.**

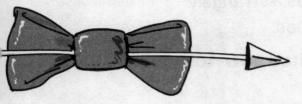

What does an archer wear
to a formal event?

**A bow tie.**

Why do archers like to meet up in
a cheese shop?

**They like to shoot the Bries.**

Which fruit is best at firing an arrow?

**A cherry.**

Did you hear the joke about the
really tall archer?

**I'm not going to bother telling
you – it'll go right over your head.**

What's an archer's favourite Queen song?

**Bow-hemian Rhapsody.**

I'm not a huge fan of archery.

**Too many drawbacks.**

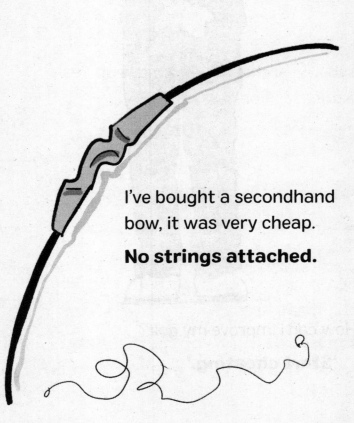

I've bought a secondhand
bow, it was very cheap.

**No strings attached.**

Always take two pairs of trousers when you play golf.

**Just in case you get a hole in one.**

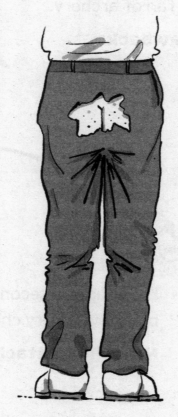

'How can I improve my golf?'

**'Start cheating.'**

How many golfers
does it take to
change
a lightbulb?

**FORE!**

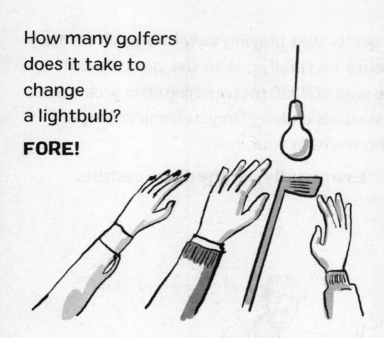

A golfing fanatic married and soon after
took his wife out for her first game. They
met a friend on the way back, who saw they
were both in a foul mood.

'What's the matter? Don't you like golf?'
asked the friend.

**'It's not fair,' said the woman.**
**'He got to hit the ball 80 or 90 times.**
**I only got to hit it 18 times.'**

A golfer was playing very badly. After many hours, he finally got to the last hole but he was still 150 metres from the green and asked his caddie, 'Do you think I can get there with a four iron?'

**'Eventually,' sighed the caddie.**

What do golfers do on Saturday night?

**Go clubbing.**

I think I've worked
out the problem
with my golf:
I'm standing too
close to the
ball . . .

**. . . after I hit it.**

After a terrible round of golf, a golfer
apologizes to her caddie. 'I've never played
that badly before,' she says.

   **'Really?' replied the caddie. 'You've
actually played before?'**

'I don't think there can possibly be a worse
golfer than me.'

   **'Oh, there are,' said the caddie. 'They
all gave up, though.'**

# On your marks, get wet, GO!

What did the coach say when his team lost in the Snake Synchronized Swimming?

**'Oh well, you can't venom all.'**

What's the biggest fear of synchronized swimmers?

**That one of the team will have a coughing fit and the rest will all copy her . . .**

What do you call a swimming
team that can't swim?

**In sink.**

Last night I dreamt I was competing
in an ocean of fizzy orange soda.

**But it was just a Fanta-sea.**

Our last competition was cancelled
when an enormous hand rose out
of the water, moved slowly
from side to side
and then disappeared.

**We were
all nearly
drowned by
a massive
wave.**

A man climbed to the
10-metre board and was
about to dive in.

'Stop!' called an umpire.
'There's no water in the pool!'

**'That's okay,'
said the
man.
'I can't
swim.'**

How do you know if a swimming pool
is safe for diving?

**It deep-ends.**

I got disqualified for weeing in the pool.

**I shouldn't have done it from
the 10-metre board.**

What do you call
a diving dog?

**A sub woofer.**

A man asks for some help in improving his
diving. Wanting to see how good he was, the
trainer takes him up to the 10-metre board
and tells him to dive in.

'This is your first time diving, isn't it?' the
trainer asks afterwards.

'Yes, how did you know?'

**'Oh . . . the wetsuit and scuba gear
kind of gave it away.'**

I wanted to try playing water polo . . .

**But I couldn't find a horse that can swim for an hour.**

What do you call a T-Rex that's really good at water polo?

**Dino-score.**

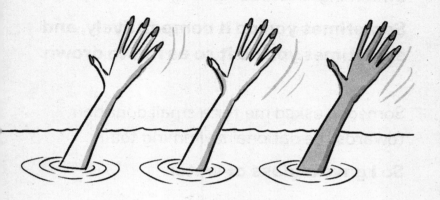

The school water-polo team were
two players short, and they were
really struggling.

**They didn't have enough boy-ancy.**

How do you start a water-polo match
between two flavours of jelly?

**'On your marks. Get set.'**

If water-polo players from Poland are
called Poles . . .

**Why aren't players from Holland
called Holes?**

Swimming is confusing.

**Sometimes you do it competitively, and sometimes you do it so as not to drown.**

Someone asked me for a small donation towards the national swimming team.

**So I gave a glass of water.**

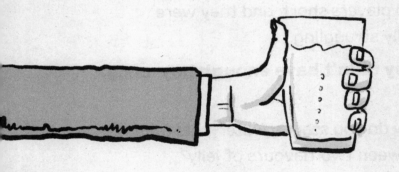

What swimming stroke can you put on toast?

**Butter-fly.**

Why did the teacher drop an exam paper in the pool?

**She wanted to test the water.**

I think my baby is going to be a great swimmer.

**He's already doing the crawl.**

Which direction do chickens swim
in their lane?

**Cluck-wise.**

What swimming stroke do sheep prefer?

**Baaackstroke.**

What race can never be run?

**A swimming race.**

Why can't two elephants go swimming
at the same time?

**Because they've only got one pair
of trunks.**

Why are spiders such good swimmers?

**Because they've got webbed feet.**

What's the best exercise for a swimmer?

**Pool-ups.**

Where do zombie swimmers train?

**The Dead Sea.**

Why shouldn't you swim on a full stomach?

**Because it's much easier to swim in water.**

Which Star Wars character loves swimming?

**Darth Wader.**

Two swimmers go to train early one morning. The first jumps straight into the pool.

'Is the water cold?' asks his friend.

'Yeah, but it feels fine after five minutes,' says the swimmer.

**'Okay, I'll wait.'**

# Pitch Puns

Why was the pig sent off the football pitch?

**For playing dirty.**

Why didn't the
dog want to
play football?

**He was a
boxer.**

Did you hear about the football team
with an invisible centre forward?

**You've never seen scoring like it.**

Why did the chicken make a nest
on the centre spot?

**She wanted to
lay it on the line.**

**'My boots are really uncomfortable.'**

'Have you got them on the right feet?'

**'Of course I have – these are the only
feet I've got.'**

How many footballers does it take to change a lightbulb?

**Just one, but you'll have to ask his agent – he arranges the transfers.**

How did the octopus save the football match?

**With his ten-tackles.**

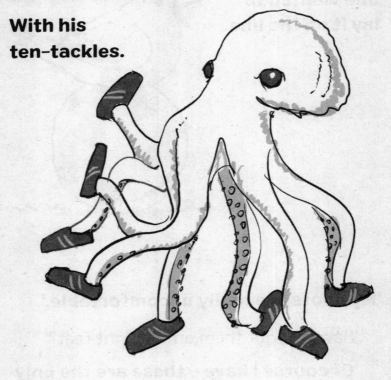

How can you tell the seabird
wasn't fit enough for football?

**It was a-puffin'.**

'Coach, I've had a great idea to improve our
chances of winning.'

**'Great – when are you leaving?'**

What drink do goalies hate?

**Penal–tea.**

What part of rugby are ghosts best at?

**Drop ghouls.**

Our referee finally retired.

**We gave him a proper send-off.**

Do you want another rugby joke?

**No thanks, I've heard a maul.**

But I've got a really good one for you!

**Yeah, nice try.**

What's a puppy's favourite sport?

**Rug-pee.**

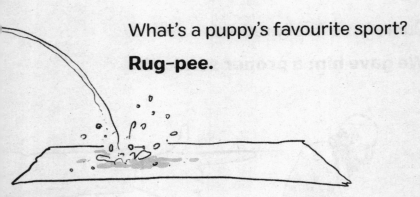

What does a rugby team taste like?

**Scrummy.**

Why don't pigs make good rugby players?

**They keep hogging the ball.**

'I've got a new rugby ball for my brother.'

**'Seems a pretty good swap.'**

Did you hear about the massive rugby player?

**He's so big, it takes him two trips to get through a revolving door.**

**Doctor:** 'That's impressive – straight off the pitch and your pulse is exactly 60 beats per minute.'

**Rugby player:** 'That's because you're feeling my watch.'

Why shouldn't you date a rugby player who just got hit in the eye?

**Not much of a catch.**

What do you call a rugby player covered in bits of grass?

**Lorna.**

**Player:** 'Why have we got to train with metre-long sticks glued to our backs?'

**Coach:** 'Because if you're going to learn anything, you have to stick to my rules.'

What do you get if you cross rugby and an invisible man?

**Rugby like no one has ever seen!**

Why are hockey players so sweaty?

**They don't have many fans.**

Which insect shouldn't play hockey?

**The fumble-bee.**

Why did the hockey player bring
an extra pair of bootlaces?

**She wanted to tie the score.**

My girlfriend's a hockey goalie.

**I think she's a keeper.**

Why didn't Cinderella qualify for the hockey team?

**She kept running away from the ball.**

Why did the pig have to stop playing hockey?

**He pulled a hamstring.**

What did one hockey ball say to the other?

**'See you round.'**

# Saddles and Wheels

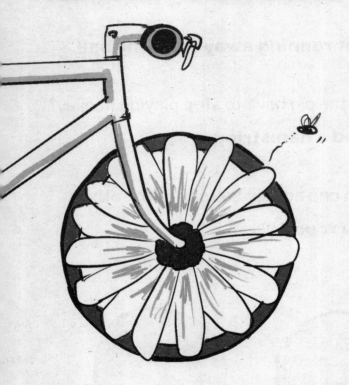

What do you get if you cross a bike
with a flower?

**Bicycle petals.**

Have you heard about the artist who makes sculptures from bicycle parts?

**He's called Cycleangelo.**

How did the barber win the cycle race?

**He took a short cut.**

What do cyclists ride in the winter?

**Icicles.**

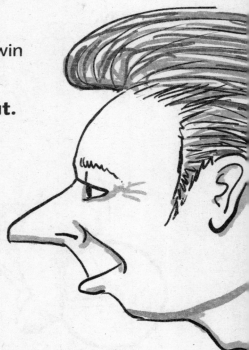

When is a bike most likely to get a puncture?

**When there's a fork in the road.**

'I heard your cycling race was a disaster – one person was going the wrong way round the track.'

**'It was much worse that that – ALL the others were going the wrong way.'**

How do you start a cycling race for bears?

**'Ready. Teddy. Go!'**

Why don't elephants
enter cycling races?

**They can't get the
helmets to fit over
their ears.**

What does a cyclist
use in their baking?

**Bike-carbonate
of soda.**

A horse walked into a restaurant.

'Hey!' shouted the waitress.

**'Ooh, yes please,' said the horse.**

What's a horse's favourite TV show?

*Neighbours.*

What's black and white and eats like a horse?

**A zebra.**

Why should you never be rude to a horse during a showjumping event?

**Because he might take offence.**

How do you spell 'hungry horse' in just four letters?

**MTGG.**

You're riding a horse at full speed, with a giraffe beside you and a lion right behind you. What do you do?

**Wait until the music stops, then get off the carousel.**

Which side of a horse has the most hair?

**The outside.**

What type of story do you tell to
a runaway horse?

**A tale of WHOA!**

Did you hear about the man who
swallowed six little plastic horses?

**The doctor said he was stable.**

What did the horse say when it fell?

**'I've fallen and I can't giddyup.'**

A rider took her injured horse to the vet. After the vet had finished the treatment, the rider asked, 'Will I be able to race him again?'

**'Yes, I think so,' said the vet. 'And you'll probably beat him.'**

Why should you worry about riding a horse after dark?

**It might be a night mare.**

Why did the rider laugh when he broke his arm?

**Because it was humerus.**


Why did the horse rider's top smell of peppermint?

**It was a Polo shirt.**


My horse's saddle is made of sandpaper.

**It's a bit of a rough ride.**

What does a skateboarder usually
say right before an accident?

**'Hey guys, watch this!'**

What's the hardest part of
learning to skateboard?

**The concrete.**

How is skateboarding like music?

**If you don't 'C sharp' you'll 'B flat'.**

How many skateboarders does it
take to change a lightbulb?

**Just one . . . but it takes at least
100 tries to get it right.**

Why do pineapples
like skateboarding?

**Because they're
hard core.**

What happened when the skateboarder got his pants caught on a wheel?

**He got his knickers in a twist.**

I'm not saying those skateboarders have a messy house . . .

**But last week vandals broke in and tidied up.**

One nervous skateboarder heard that most accidents happen at home.

**So he moved.**

What's the difference between a short plank on wheels, and a flat fish waiting ages for a bus?

**One's a bored skate, the other's a skateboard.**

# One on One

Judo is basically the art of folding clothes . . .

**. . . While people are still wearing them.**

Why did the judo player stand on his head?

**He was turning things over
in his mind.**

What did the mussel do when she won
her judo match?

**She shell-ebrated.**

What do you say when King Kong
wins a judo match?

**'Kong-ratulations.'**

What medicines do karate players
take to avoid getting punched?

**Antifistamines.**

I was threatened by a bully last week.

'I'm warning you!' I said. 'I know taekwondo!'

**He got scared and left, which was lucky – I don't know any other Korean words.**

What form of martial art do soya beans prefer?

**To-fu.**

Two taekwondo players have competed together their whole lives. When one of them died suddenly, his grieving friend dedicated his next match to his sparring partner: 'I hope there's taekwondo in heaven.'

That night, his dead friend appears in a dream. 'I have good news and bad news,' the ghost says. 'The good news is there really is taekwondo in heaven.'

'Really? That's great. So what's the bad news?'

**'You're fighting tomorrow.'**

Why did the cupboard learn taekwondo?

**For shelf-defence.**

My martial arts trainer brought cupcakes for the class.

**He told us we could only Taek-won-do.**

Why is fencing the best sport?

**All the others are pointless.**

I don't want to talk about how I lost my fencing match.

**It's still a sore subject.**

'Do you like fencing?'

**'Sword of.'**

My grandad was a champion fencer.

**He built one right round his garden
in just one day. Amazing.**

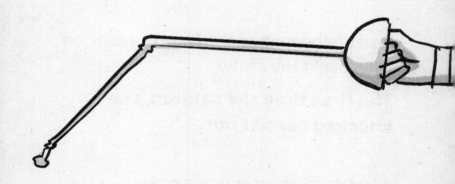

I had to give up fencing.

**I just couldn't see the
point anymore.**

What do you call a pig that does karate?

**Porkchop.**

What happened to the karate champion who joined the army?

**The first time she saluted, she knocked herself out.**

A karate instructor was arrested after leaving a shopping centre.

**He was caught chop lifting.**

I'm not actually that fond of karate.

**I just really hate planks of wood.**

My friend was confronted in a dark alley but thought he could beat the muggers because he knew karate.

**Unfortunately, his wallet was taken while he was still taking his shoes and socks off.**

How many wrestling fans does it take to change a lightbulb?

**Both of them.**

Two silkworms had a wrestling match.

**It ended in a tie.**

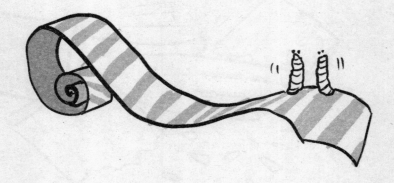

Did you hear about the wrestling egg?

**He got beaten.**

I was watching wrestling on TV the other day.

**It was gripping.**

'Why are you wrestling with the Christmas decorations?'

'Because you said I needed to take them down.'

73

I think I may be a bit unfit.

**I tried mud wrestling . . . and the mud won.**

My wife left me because I'm a compulsive liar.

**At least, I think that's what she said –
I didn't really hear because I was
wrestling a tiger.**

I've been trying to meet up with my wrestling friend, but it's difficult to agree a date.

**He's very hard to pin down.**

What's the difference between wrestlers on TV and professional footballers?

**The wrestlers will get up after faking an injury.**

I met a wrestler with a book where he kept photos of his fights.

**It was a scrapbook.**

Can a match box?

**No, but a tin can.**

Why do boxers have 'TGIF' written
on their shoes?

**Toes Go In First.**

What do you call the boxer who comes
last in a competition?

**A sore loser.**

What do you call an ordinary potato
that talks about a boxing match?

**The common tater.**

A boxer goes to her doctor, complaining she can't get to sleep.

'Have you tried counting sheep?' asks the doctor.

**'It doesn't work,' says the boxer. 'Every time I get to "nine", I get up.'**

Why are boxers so funny?

**They love a punch line.**

'Coach, my sparring partner has called in sick. Shall I train on my own?'

**'Why not – knock yourself out.'**

When is a boxing match like a crossword puzzle?

**When you start vertical and end up horizontal.**

Did you hear about the boxing pirate?

**He had a mean left hook.**

What kind of punch does a boxer dog use?

**A puppercut.**

Did you hear the joke about ten boxers in a row?

**This is the punchline.**

The confident amateur boxer was about to fight a brilliant professional.

'I think I can beat that guy blindfolded!' he boasts.

**'Maybe,' says his coach. 'But what if he's not blindfolded?'**

Why was the terrible boxer nicknamed 'The Artist'?

**Because he spent most of his time on the canvas.**

A boxer started her match swinging furiously, but didn't land a single punch on her opponent.

'How am I doing?' she asks her coach at the end of a round.

**'If you keep this up,' replies the coach, 'she might catch a cold from the draft.'**

What do you call a monkey that wins a boxing match?

**Chimp-ion.**

# Solo Efforts

What's the difference between a bad golfer and a bad climber?

**The golfer WHACKS then says 'Oops', whilst the climber says 'Oops' then goes WHACK.**

What's the difference between a climbing fan and a pension?

**Eventually, a pension will mature and make some money.**

'Mum, when I grow up I want to be a rock climber!'

**'Well, dear, you can't do both.'**

What did the climber say to the very high wall?

**'I don't like your altitude.'**

A guide was explaining a route to a group of mountain climbers.

'Depending on your skill, the ascent could take anywhere between one and two hours,' he said. **'And the descent could take anywhere between 30 minutes and 30 seconds.'**

A weightlifter and their partner were training by lifting tiny 1-kilo weights.

**The weightlifter turned to their partner and said, 'I don't think this is really working out.'**

What do you call a row of weightlifters?

**A pick-up line.**

Have you heard about the weightlifting physicist?

**He trained by pumping ion.**

If you want to lift using a ten-metre-long bar . . .

**You're going to have a long weight.**

**Trainer:** 'Come on! You can do it! Give it all you've got!'

**Weightlifter:** 'Can I please just go to the loo in peace?'

Did you hear about the weightlifting farmer?

**He had enormous calves.**

What exercise do zombie weightlifters do?

**The deadlift.**

Which vegetable is best at weightlifting?

**Muscle sprouts.**

Why did the fish stop lifting weights?

**It pulled a mussel.**

What's the difference between a Scottish taxi and a weedy weightlifter?

**One's got wee cabs, and the other's got weak abs.**

It's hard to join the gymnastics team.

**You have to bend over backwards to get in.**

Where do cheating gymnasts end up?

**Behind parallel bars.**

Why do gymnasts season their food more in August?

**They love to summer-salt.**

I used to be terrified of the vaulting horse.

**But eventually I got over it.**

Sometimes I like to tuck my knees
in to my chest and lean forwards.

**It's just how I roll.**

I've been terrible at gymnastics since
I spent too much and got overdrawn.

**I've lost my balance.**

How can you
tell if a girl
really enjoys
trampolining?

**She's head
over heels!**

I forgot to tell my
husband I swapped
our bed for a trampoline.

**He went through the roof.**

'I'm worried my trampoline is sick.'

**'Don't worry, it'll bounce back.'**

What's the best time to use a trampoline?
**Spring.**

I used to work as a trampoline tester.

**The job had its ups and downs.**

What do you get if you cross a cow with
a trampoline?

**A milkshake.**

I bounced so high on the trampoline . . .

**I came down with snow on my head.**

'That blind athlete was very impressive on the trampoline, wasn't he?'

**'Yes . . . the guide dog looked a bit stressed, though.'**

# Out on the Water

Why did the Bluetooth speakers lose their rowing race?

**They kept trying to sync.**

How do pirates measure how far they've rowed?

**In yarrrrds.**

How do you make a rowing boat
look younger?

**Boat-tox.**

My rowing team was terrible last year, but
this season we've been even worse.

**We've sunk to new lows.**

What did the gold-medal winners
call their quad?

**Usain Boat.**

Why did the surfer cross the beach?

**To get to the other tide.**

How do surfers stay clean?

**They wash up on the beach.**

How do surfers greet each other?

**With a massive wave.**

Where does music go surfing?

**On sound waves.**

**Surfer 1:** 'What's the difference between ignorance and indifference?'

**Surfer 2:** 'I don't know, and I don't care.'

What does an animal doctor wear to surf?

**A vetsuit.**

What did the wave say to the surfer?

**'Have a swell time!'**

My boyfriend showed me two kayak paddles and asked me to pick one.

**I said I'd take either oar.**

If you're kayaking in winter, don't light a fire to keep warm – however cold it gets.

**You can't have your kayak and heat it.**

I need to sell my canoe equipment after my dog did a wee on it.

**I've got to peddle a poodle-piddle paddle.**

It was really busy and crowded when the sports shop had a sale on canoe equipment.

**It was quite an oar-deal.**

The kayak race was abandoned when a truckload of terrapins were accidentally spilt in the river.

**It was a turtle disaster.**

What does Donald Trump call
artificial kayaks?

**'Fake canoes!'**

What is a cow's favourite water sport?

**Ca–MOO–ing.**

I am always rowing with my wife.

**We really love our kayak.**

**Knock knock!**

Who's there?

**Canoe.**

Canoe who?

**Canoe think of any more kayak jokes?**

That boat is getting very close to shore,
we should run away.

**It's ready for a tack.**

What did the sea say to the sailing boat?
**Nothing, it just waved.**

What's it called when bigger boats
bully smaller boats?
**Pier pressure.**

Where do sick catamarans go?

**To the dock.**

I started a successful business
building dinghies in my attic.

**Sails are through the roof.**

# Nets and Balls

Why is badminton so noisy?

**Every player raises a racket.**

My dog, Minton, just ate all my shuttlecocks.

**Bad Minton!**

My friends don't get my badminton jokes.

**I don't think they appreciate my shuttle humour.**

WACK

Some people don't like badminton.

**They think it's a bit wacky.**

My mate suggested we play doubles badminton.

**It was no good though – we couldn't find two people that looked exactly like us.**

Which animal is best at beach volleyball?

**The score-pion.**

What do you call a girl standing in
the middle of a volleyball court?

**Annette.**

I got forced to play volleyball, but
I wasn't very good at serving the ball.

**It didn't go over very well.**

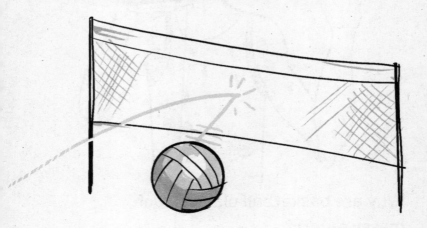

How do you know if the opposing
team doesn't like your serve?

**They keep returning it.**

Why don't volleyball players make good
restaurant employees?

**They get confused when asked to
serve food.**

Why are basketball players such messy eaters?

**They're always dribbling.**

What does a basketball player do when they lose their eyesight?

**They become a referee.**

Why is the basketball arena so hot after the game finishes?

**Because all the fans have left.**

Why can't basketball players go on holiday?

**They aren't allowed to travel.**

Why are basketball players respected?

**Because everyone looks up to them.**

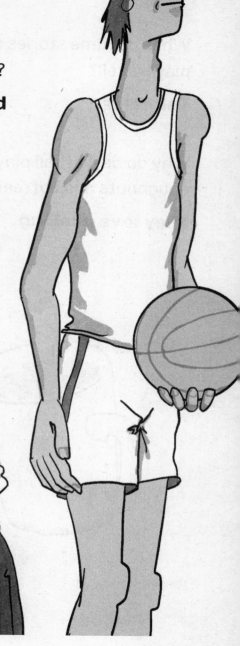

What bedtime stories do basketball players tell?

**Tall tales.**

Why do basketball players like doughnuts and coffee?

**They love dunking.**

Why was the chicken kicked off
the basketball team?

**For persistent fowl play.**

What did the bee say when he sank his shot?

**'Hive scored!'**

What part of a basketball arena
is never the same?

**The changing rooms.**

What do you serve but not eat?

**A table-tennis ball.**

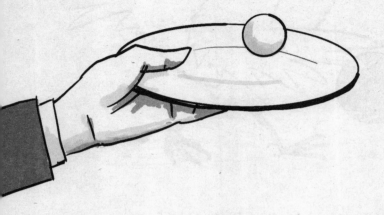

Why are fish no good at table tennis?

**They don't like getting close to the net.**

When do table-tennis players go to bed?

**Tennish.**

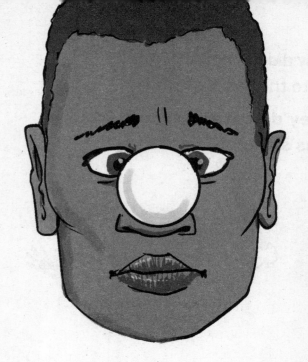

I wasn't sure why the table-tennis ball kept getting bigger.

**Then it hit me.**

What do you call an argument about table tennis?

**A ping pong ding-dong.**

Why did the police officers go to the baseball game?

**They'd heard someone was stealing a base.**

How many baseball players does it take to change a lightbulb?

**No one knows. They're still arguing whose fault it was the bulb stopped working.**

What did the baseball glove say to the ball?

**Catch you later.**

What do cupcakes and softball teams have in common?

**They both depend on the batter.**

What runs all the way round a baseball field but never moves?

**The fence.**

Why don't matches play baseball?

**One strike and they're out.**

Did you hear the joke about the softball?

**It'll leave you in stitches.**

Why do singers make good softball players?

**They have perfect pitch.**

Why is baseball played at night?

**Because the bats sleep during the day.**

Which superhero is best at baseball?

**Batman.**

Have you ever played silent tennis?

**It's just like normal tennis, but without the racket.**

Why should you never marry a tennis player?

**Because to them, 'love' means nothing.**

The neighbours are annoyed I've started making tennis equipment in my garage.

**They said they'll report me for making a racket.**

I'm happy to give you my old tennis racket.

**No strings attached.**

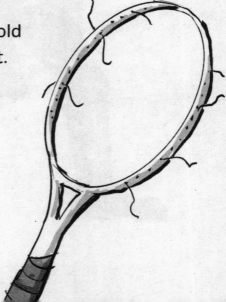

I went to the wedding of two tennis players...

**It was a beautiful service.**

A tennis ball walks into a restaurant.

**The waiter asks, 'Have you been served?'**

Apparently, I'm too indecisive to be a
tennis umpire . . .

**But I still haven't ruled it out.**

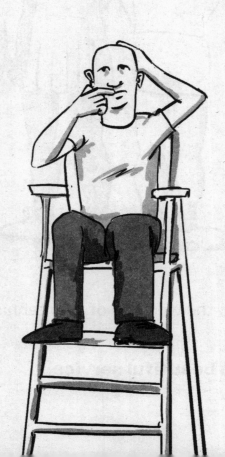

Why do waiters make good tennis players?

**Because they're such excellent servers.**

What has 4 legs and grunts?

**A doubles tennis team.**

Did you hear about the naughty
tennis ball that got arrested?

**It's waiting to go to court.**

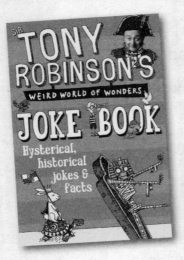

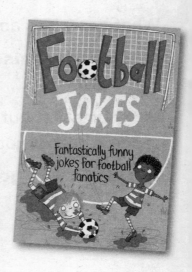

**What's black and white and will have you in stitches?**